For My Sons

Once upon a time,
long ago and far away,
a little shark named Otis
packed his bags and went away.

His Mom and Dad were fearsome sharks,
they loved Otis a bunch.
They showed him how to catch big fish,
and shrimp and crabs for lunch.

But his parents were annoying.
He should be free to roam.
So he waved goodbye to all his friends,
and left behind his ocean home.

His parents tried to stop him.
They begged him not to go.
But Otis said, "I'm leaving.
A little shark needs room to grow."

So he swam for miles and miles
until he couldn't see his home.
Then he swam up to a little beach
where he thought he was alone.

But there was a big, fat frog
who sat there catching flies,
with his slimy, sticky tongue
and his big, fat, bulging eyes.

"Excuse me, Mr. Frog,"
said Otis as he swam.
"Could you help a shark who's lost?
Because that is what I am."

The frog looked down at Otis
with one big, fat, bulging eye
and said, "This beach belongs to me,
so you'll have to go now. Goodbye!"

So Otis swam a little more
looking for some food to take.
And basking on the rocky shore
he saw a garden snake.

"Pardon me," said Otis,
just as nicely as he could.
"I'm looking for a place to live.
Can I stay here? I'll be good."

The snake just looked at Otis
and said, "I'm sorry. You can't stay.
Little sharks do not belong here,
so you'll have to go away."

So Otis swam away again,
not quite knowing what to do.
He was tired, sad, and lonely…
and he was getting hungry, too.

He swam up to a seashell,
searching for some lunch to grab.
When all at once, there it was…
Little Otis spied a crab!

He swam up to the little crab
and was just about to eat,
but the crab begged, "Please let me go,
and I'll promise you a treat."

Otis was very hungry,
and a treat sounded pretty good.
So he let the crab go free
to bring back what treats he could.

But when the crab returned,
he brought no treat or snack.
Instead he went and got more crabs…
And brought an army back!

A thousand angry crabs
all pinching with their claws.
So Otis swam away to find
Something else to fill his jaws.

He came into a darkened cave
and stopped to look around.
He had hoped to find some fish to eat,
But there was nothing to be found.

Then Otis heard an awful noise…
a rumbling way down deep.
He had awoken a giant octopus
from the comfort of its sleep!

Otis knew he was in trouble,
and he knew that it was bad.
So he did the only thing he could…
He cried out for his dad.

And from far across the ocean
his father heard his call,
and came speeding to his rescue
without any fear at all.

The octopus let Otis go
When he saw the big shark come,
And said, "I beg your pardon,
I didn't know he was your son."

Little Otis missed his mom and dad.
He didn't want to be alone.
So he gave his dad a hug and said,
"I'm sorry, dad. Let's go home!"

Made in the USA
Middletown, DE
18 December 2017